by Tracey West and Katherine Noll
illustrated by Aly Michalka

GROSSET & DUNLAP
Published by the Penguin Group
Penguin Group (USA) Inc., 375 Hudson Street, New York, New York 10014, USA
Penguin Group (Canada), 90 Eglinton Avenue East, Suite 700,
Toronto, Ontario M4P 2Y3, Canada
(a division of Pearson Penguin Canada Inc.)
Penguin Books Ltd., 80 Strand, London WC2R 0RL, England
Penguin Group Ireland, 25 St. Stephen's Green, Dublin 2, Ireland
(a division of Penguin Books Ltd.)
Penguin Group (Australia), 250 Camberwell Road, Camberwell, Victoria 3124, Australia
(a division of Pearson Australia Group Pty. Ltd.)
Penguin Books India Pvt. Ltd., 11 Community Centre, Panchsheel Park,
New Delhi—110 017, India
Penguin Group (NZ), 67 Apollo Drive, Rosedale, North Shore 0632, New Zealand
(a division of Pearson New Zealand Ltd.)
Penguin Books (South Africa) (Pty.) Ltd., 24 Sturdee Avenue,
Rosebank, Johannesburg 2196, South Africa

Penguin Books Ltd., Registered Offices:
80 Strand, London WC2R 0RL, England

Cover photo courtesy of Joe Magnani.

Copyright © 2008 by FREAKY TWIN POWER. All rights reserved. Published by
Grosset & Dunlap, a division of Penguin Young Readers Group, 345 Hudson Street, New
York, New York 10014. GROSSET & DUNLAP is a trademark of Penguin Group (USA) Inc.
Manufactured in China.

Library of Congress Cataloging-in-Publication Data is available.

ISBN 978-0-448-44844-2   10 9 8 7 6 5 4 3 2 1

CHAPTER ONE:
NEXT STOP, SEATTLE

"Thank you." AJ smiled as the flight attendant handed her a bottle of water.

"Would your sister like something to drink?" asked the flight attendant, whose name tag said KAREN.

AJ glanced at Aly. She was curled up in her window seat, her eyes closed and the hood of her sweatshirt pulled up over her head, with a few stray blond curls poking out.

"Aly?" AJ reached over and tapped her sister. Aly muttered and turned in her seat.

Her eyes popped open and she looked at AJ.

"What?" Aly practically shouted.

AJ reached over and yanked Aly's hood off her head. Her iPod was in her ear.

Aly grinned. "Oops, sorry," she said. She took the earpiece out and sat up straight. She gave a big yawn and stretched her arms.

"Would you like something to drink, miss?" Karen asked.

"Yes, please," Aly answered. "Water would be great. My throat is so dry."

Karen handed her a bottle of water and a plastic cup. She smiled. "We can't have that! It's not every day I have two famous singers on my flight. You need to keep your voice in good shape. Aren't you going to be performing at a concert in Seattle?"

AJ nodded. "We are, but we've got other business in Seattle, too."

"We're going to be judges in a contest for young songwriters," Aly added. "So we had to get to town early. That means we got to fly out and take a break from the tour bus."

Karen smiled. "Well, if you need anything at all, let me know," she said. Then she moved down the plane's narrow aisle with her drink cart.

AJ leaned back against her seat. "I kind of miss the bus," she said. "And all of our Hello Kitty stuff."

"I know what you mean," Aly said. "The bus does feel like home. But you know how I start to get bus crazy!"

AJ laughed. "You're like a bird trapped in a cage. I'm sure the guys in the band are happy to have the bus to themselves for this trip."

"And I'm so totally stoked about judging this contest. We'll get to hear all the young, hot talent that's out there," Aly said. "The winner even gets a college scholarship! It's awesome that we get to give out a huge prize like that."

"We'd better pick someone really good. We're going to be performing one of the winner's songs at our concert at KeyArena," AJ reminded her.

"We'll need extra rehearsal time with the band to learn the new song," Aly said. "We'd better remind Jim to work the extra time into our schedule."

AJ laughed. "This is Jim we're talking about, remember?" she said. Jim, their tour manager, was right out of college. Even though he was young, he was more organized than anyone they'd ever met.

AJ suddenly got a nervous look on her face. "I am worried about one thing," she said. "If we're judges, we'll have to tell people if we don't like their songs. You know what it's like when we write songs for our albums. They're like little pieces of our souls, practically. I don't want to break anyone's heart."

"We just have to be careful what we say," Aly suggested. "Sometimes we get constructive criticism from our producer, or even each other.

We'll just focus on what works and try to give them some pointers for the rest."

AJ relaxed. "You're right. It's not like we have to be mean or anything!"

"And the songwriters have already been narrowed down to twelve finalists. They must be pretty talented to have made it that far," Aly added. "I heard that thousands of people entered."

AJ pulled her notebook out from where she had stashed it in the little pocket in the seat in front of her. She unclipped a pen from the binder.

Aly giggled. "AJ, you would be lost without your notebook!"

AJ grinned sheepishly. "It makes me feel better to write things down. It helps me to stay organized. Now," she said as she began to write, "we'll listen to the twelve finalists in the first round. Then we'll have to cut six right away!" She looked up from her notebook. "That's a lot."

"There can only be one winner," Aly said.

"At some point, they'll all be eliminated except for one."

"Okay," AJ said as she started to write again. "Then we'll have to narrow down the six contestants to three. And out of that final three we'll pick the winner."

"It's a big responsibility," Aly said. "But I'm sure we'll pick someone awesome."

She gave a little dry cough. AJ shook her head. "Karen was right. You've got to drink your water and take care of your voice," she said. "By the end of the week, we'll be singing in Seattle!"

AMBER

CHAPTER TWO:
WINNERS AND LOSERS

After the plane landed, the girls had to race to their next destination. They were used to it by now. Being on the road meant they were always rushing off somewhere.

They waited for their luggage, then for a car to take them to their hotel to drop off their bags. They quickly changed, then stopped by the hotel's coffee bar to pick up a couple of lattes. The driver whisked them off to a theater in downtown Seattle.

"Ahhh," AJ took a deep breath of the steamy coffee concoction. "This hits the spot."

They were sitting in red velvet theater seats. The stage was empty, but they could hear noises coming from backstage. The twelve finalists were getting ready to perform their best songs in front of Aly and AJ.

A petite young woman with long reddish-blond hair walked over to them. She carried a clipboard and a stack of papers. "Aly, AJ," she said as she held out her hand to them. "My name is Lily. I work for Entertainment Unlimited, one of the companies sponsoring the competition. I'm the contest coordinator."

Aly and AJ shook hands with her.

"We're really excited to be here," Aly said.

"If you think you're excited, you should see the contestants," Lily said. "They can't wait to perform. The first person will take the stage in just a few minutes. Can I get you anything?"

Aly gestured to her coffee. "We're good."

"Let me leave you with these." Lily handed them each a bundle of papers. "It has the contestants' names, ages, and what they'll be singing. Most of the performers have taped music that we'll be playing to accompany them, but a few will be playing guitars."

"Thanks, Lily," AJ said.

Lily disappeared backstage. AJ took her notebook out from her purse.

"I'm ready!" she joked.

"I won't laugh," Aly said. "Look what I've got!" She pulled a notebook out from her own bag. "I figured we'd both need to take notes while we were judging."

"See—you are finally beginning to understand the beauty of the notebook." AJ laughed.

Aly reached into her bag again.

"Uh, AJ," she said. "I got the notebook but forgot to bring a pen!"

"Don't worry," AJ grabbed an extra from her purse. "I'm always prepared."

They settled back as the first contestant walked onstage. It was a teenage girl dressed all in black, with black lipstick and makeup. She had dark hair that she wore up in a spiky ponytail. She stepped up to the microphone.

"My name is Amber," she said. "I'll be singing my song, 'Rain of Tears.'"

The song was a little depressing, but Aly and AJ were impressed with the melody and the thoughtful lyrics.

Next, a boy named Henry came out. He was tall and thin with big, dark eyes. He sang a love song while he strummed an acoustic guitar. Henry was followed by a boy named Kurt who sang a country song, and a long-haired girl named Rainbow who sang a folk song. Each contestant was different in his or her own way. Aly and AJ carefully wrote down their impressions of everybody who performed.

A girl walked shyly out onto the stage. She wore her long red hair braided down her back, and she carried an acoustic guitar. She shuffled to the microphone, staring at her feet.

"I'm Claire," she said softly into the microphone. "And I'll be singing 'Lost.'"

Claire's low voice could barely be heard, and Aly and AJ had to strain to be able to hear the lyrics. She sang about feeling alone and confused, but finding strength inside herself. The girls liked the lyrics they heard, and they were touched by the haunting and beautiful melody.

"Wow!" AJ said. "She was great, but she's so shy!"

Aly nodded. "I wish she would have sung louder."

The next contestant was Claire's exact opposite. He carried an acoustic guitar, too. But while Claire was timid, Austin walked out like he owned the theater. He flashed a huge smile at Aly and AJ.

"Hey, great to meet you," he said. "It's not every day I get to sing for two gorgeous babes."

Aly chuckled and nudged AJ in the ribs with her elbow. Austin, with his dark blue eyes and brown hair, was cute, but he was laying it on thick.

He confidently began to strum his guitar. Aly and AJ were expecting a corny song, but Austin surprised them by singing about a girl who only pretended to be in love with him. His lyrics were intelligent and the song had a great hook. The whole time he was singing, he stared at AJ. Once, he even winked at her.

He took a bow when he was done.

"I wrote that song from a real experience," he said. "But AJ, I was thinking you might be the perfect girl to help mend my broken heart."

"Thanks, Austin," AJ smiled. "But I'm here to judge the contest, not date the contestants."

"If you change your mind, I'll come running," Austin vowed.

Aly and AJ looked at each other and began to crack up as Austin left the stage.

A girl named Bree who belted out a bluesy tune wowed them. The next contestant, Heather, wasn't as good. Her song was decent, but bland.

Then Josh took the stage. He looked sharp in jeans, a fitted T-shirt, and a blazer. As soon as the music started, Aly and AJ were impressed. The melody was fresh and original, but at the same time very catchy. Then Josh began to sing.

"You loved me, but then you had to flee," Josh sang. Aly and AJ grimaced. His lyrics were very corny.

The last three contestants came out and performed. Now Aly and AJ had to make a tough decision.

"Only six can go to the next round," Aly said.

"Hmmm," AJ said as she looked over her notes. "I like Amber's song a lot."

"It was kind of dark," Aly said. "But good. I

say she goes through. Now what about your new boyfriend, Austin?"

AJ laughed. "Could you believe him? What a flirt!"

"And he was good. He's got real talent. He doesn't need to butter up the judges," Aly said with a laugh.

"Claire's song was the best, lyrically, I'd say," AJ said. "But she was so timid onstage. I could barely hear her."

"But this is a songwriting contest, not a singing contest," Aly pointed out.

"You're right," AJ agreed. "Then she should definitely go through."

Aly looked down at her notes. "I'm not so sure about Josh," Aly said. "His melody was fantastic, but those lyrics . . ."

"Need work!" AJ finished. "But his melody was off the hook. I could totally imagine us performing that onstage."

They continued to debate about who the final six should be. After a few minutes, the girls looked at their list.

"It's a good thing we think alike," Aly remarked. "I'm glad we didn't have to argue about anybody."

"It's early in the contest, though," AJ teased. "What if we each want a different person to win?"

Aly's eyes widened. "Oh, no. I didn't think of that!" she said.

"Don't worry," AJ said. "We can always arm wrestle to decide the winner. But I should warn you, I've been working out." She flexed her arm to show off her muscle, laughing.

Lily walked up. "Ready?" she asked. "I'll call the contestants to the stage."

Aly and AJ nodded. They were excited, but they felt bad at the same time. Even though they were about to make six people very happy, they were also going to disappoint six more.

The boys and girls filed out onto the stage.

Lily brought the microphone over to Aly and AJ.

"First of all, we want to thank you all so much for performing for us," Aly began. "We enjoyed every single song. You are a group of extremely talented young artists and our decision was very difficult." She handed the microphone to AJ.

"I'm going to read the names of the people who will continue in the competition," AJ said. She held a piece of paper in front of her. "Austin," she said. He let out a cheer and began dancing around the stage. AJ had to wait for him to quiet down before she could continue. "Bree, Henry, Amber, Claire, and Josh. We'd like for all of you to compete in the next round. To everybody who didn't make it, thanks again. You were all really great. Keep writing songs! You've all got talent."

Some of the contestants exchanged hugs. A few were crying. Then one of the contestants, Heather, stomped up to the front of the stage.

"This is a total rip-off!" she screamed at the

contestants around her. They slowly backed away. "I was robbed! You guys call yourselves songwriters? My dog could write better songs than you!"

"Sounds like someone is a sore loser," Austin smirked.

"Whatever! My song was the best and I know it." She turned and glared at Aly and AJ. "You made a big mistake, I hope you realize that. This contest is a joke without me in it." Then she stomped off of the stage.

Aly and AJ were shocked.

"Wow," Aly said finally.

"Too bad she didn't put that kind of energy into her song," AJ said, shaking her head. "She might have made it to the finals."

CHAPTER THREE:
A MISSING NOTEBOOK

The contestants all headed backstage.

"Maybe we should go talk to them," Aly suggested. "I want to make sure that the other kids aren't as upset as Heather."

"Good idea," AJ agreed.

The cramped backstage area was a mess of folding tables and benches. The contestants' guitar cases and other belongings were strewn all over. They spotted Austin talking excitedly to goth-looking Amber. They looked happy. In another corner, the country singer Kurt and the folksinger Rainbow were hugging each other.

"Let's go talk to them," Aly said.

They approached the two songwriters. "Hey, Kurt. Hey, Rainbow," AJ began. "We just wanted to say that both of you have a lot of talent."

"You should definitely keep writing songs," Aly told them.

Rainbow nodded. "Thanks," she said. "It would have been really cool to win. But somebody has to lose, right?"

"I just wish it wasn't us," Kurt said with a sad smile.

"And don't let Heather bother you," Rainbow added. "She's, like, super-dramatic."

The sisters thanked them and headed over to Claire. She was standing over her open guitar case, with her back to Aly and AJ.

"Hi, Claire," AJ said. "We just wanted to

say congratulations. We really liked your song."

Claire didn't answer. Aly and AJ exchanged glances, then moved in closer. Claire was softly crying.

"Claire, what's wrong?" Aly asked.

Claire straightened up and wiped the tears from her cheeks. "It's my notebook," she said, between sobs. "It's not here."

"It's probably around here somewhere," AJ said. "We can help you look for it. What does it look like?"

Claire took a deep breath. "I'm sorry I'm freaking out," she said. "Every song I've ever written is in that notebook. I'm really happy that you picked me to move on in the contest. But without my notebook, I won't have anything to present in the next round."

"I can totally relate," AJ said. "Sometimes I think I'd be lost without my notebook. But I'm sure yours is around here somewhere."

"It's purple," Claire said. "And there's a picture of a butterfly that I pasted onto it. I always keep it inside my guitar case. But when I opened my case just now to put my guitar back, the notebook was gone."

"Maybe it fell out," Aly suggested. She knelt down and looked under the bench. She spotted some dust bunnies and a chewed-up pencil, but no notebook.

"Keep looking," AJ told Aly. "I'm going to ask around and see if anyone has seen it."

Aly scanned the backstage area. Most of the contestants had left already. She cornered Kurt and Rainbow as they were about to leave. Neither of them had seen the notebook.

Austin and Amber were packing up their things.

"Congratulations, guys," she said. "Aly and I really liked your songs."

"Cool," Amber said. She had a nice smile that somehow didn't match all of her black makeup.

"Thanks," Austin replied, grinning at AJ. "But

you know, you might as well not bother with the next round. You've got your winner right here."

AJ shook her head, but she couldn't help smiling back. Austin was cocky, but there was something really sweet about him, too.

"We'll see about that," she said. "Listen, have either of you seen a purple notebook back here? Claire lost hers."

"No," Amber replied.

"That's too bad," Austin said. "So, what number should I call you at if I find it?"

"You can call Lily," AJ said. This boy was persistent!

Austin reached into his own guitar case and took out a blue flyer. He handed it to AJ. "If you and Aly aren't doing anything tomorrow night, you should check out this poetry slam," he said. "The best poets in Seattle will be there. That includes me, of course. Actually, a lot of the contestants are part of the poetry scene."

"That sounds cool," AJ said. She had heard about poetry slams before, when poets get up onstage and read their poems to an audience. She'd always wanted to go to one. "Maybe we'll see you tomorrow."

"I know you will," Austin said.

Amber rolled her eyes. "Austin, give it a rest."

AJ laughed and headed back to Aly and Claire. "Any luck?" she asked.

"Nothing," Aly replied. "How about you?"

"Nobody's seen anything," AJ said. "But then again, I didn't get a chance to talk to everybody. Maybe something will turn up."

Claire looked like she might cry again.

"Claire, do you have a copy of your songs somewhere? On a computer, maybe?" Aly asked.

"No," Claire said. "I know I should have. But the notebook's all I've got."

Aly gave her a hug. "You'll find it. We'll talk to Lily for you. She can have the theater manager look for it."

"It's a few days until the next round," AJ reminded her. "I'm sure it will turn up before then."

Claire nodded. "Thanks."

She packed up her guitar case and left, casting a sad glance around the room before she went through the door. Aly and AJ were alone backstage now.

"I feel so bad for her," Aly said. "I hope it turns up."

"I do, too," AJ said. "But I have a feeling—"

"Oh, no," Aly interrupted. "I know what you're thinking. This is another mystery, isn't it?"

"It could be," AJ said. "There is a big prize for the winner of this contest. Maybe one of the contestants stole Claire's notebook so they'd have a better chance of winning. See how upset she got? I wouldn't be surprised if she dropped out."

Aly sighed and sat down on a bench. "I hate to admit it, but I think you're right," she said. "I guess we've reached the next stop on the Aly and AJ Mystery Tour!"

CHAPTER FOUR:
SIGHTSEEING IN SEATTLE

"Look! A coffee shop! Can we please stop?"

Aly watched the coffee shop disappear into the distance as the car sped past it.

"Oh, come on, Jim," she moaned. "We were on a plane all day yesterday. Then we spent all night judging that contest. I feel like I barely slept last night! A latte would really help right now."

"Definitely," AJ agreed, yawning.

Their tour manager looked into the rearview

mirror. Jim's light brown eyes sparkled with amusement.

"Sorry, but your tour of the Space Needle starts in ten minutes," Jim reminded them.

The girls' mom turned to look at them from the passenger seat. Carrie never seemed to look tired, no matter how little sleep she got.

"We're very lucky to get this special tour," she told them. "I remember taking you girls to the top of the tower when you were little. We waited more than an hour in line!"

"I think I remember that," Aly said. "I was scared to go in the elevator."

AJ frowned. "I don't have any memories of the Space Needle at all." Two years younger than Aly, she had been very young when her family moved from Seattle to California.

"Well, today we'll have to create some new memories," Carrie said. "I've got my camera!"

The sisters looked at each other and smiled.

Their mom's positive attitude was contagious, even when they were feeling tired.

"Look, we're almost there," Jim said.

The tall, metal tower was visible from most points in Seattle. Now that they were close, they had to crane their necks to get a good look at it. The round observation deck sat on top of the tall steel tower.

"It almost looks like a flying saucer up there," Aly remarked.

"Maybe that's why they call it the Space Needle," AJ guessed.

Jim parked the car, and they were met at the elevator entrance by a young woman with a bright smile.

"Aly and AJ," she said. "Welcome back to Seattle. I'm a fan of yours, you know. Your new album rocks."

AJ shook her hand. "Thanks . . ."

The woman laughed. "Oh, sorry. My name is

Malika. I work for the Space Needle Corporation. I'll be giving you a tour today."

"We're really excited about this," Carrie said. "Thank you for arranging it for us."

"No problem," Malika said. "Follow me."

She led them past the line of tourists and stopped by the elevator door.

AJ grinned at Aly. "Still scared?" she teased.

"I think I'll be okay," her sister replied dryly.

"It takes forty-one seconds to get to the top," Malika explained. "The Space Needle is six hundred feet high—about the same height as a sixty-story building."

"Why did they build a tower this high?" AJ asked.

"The Space Needle was built as an attraction for the 1962 World's Fair," Malika said. "From the Observation Deck, there is a view of downtown Seattle, plus some of the most beautiful mountain ranges in the Pacific Northwest."

"I think there have been some changes since the last time we visited here," Carrie said. "Isn't there a restaurant at the top?"

Malika nodded. "It rotates, so diners can get a full three-hundred-and-sixty-degree view while they're eating."

"I think that would make me dizzy," Aly said.

"It rotates very slowly," Malika explained.

The elevator doors opened, and they stepped inside. The elevator walls were clear.

"Keep your eyes open," Malika told them. "Some people say the elevator ride is the best part of the visit."

The doors closed, and the elevator motor hummed as the elevator began its rise hundreds of feet in the air. Soon the girls could see the morning sun shimmering on beautiful blue water.

"That's Puget Sound, an arm of the Pacific Ocean," Malika said.

In the next moments, a majestic snow-covered mountain peak came into view.

"Mount Rainier," Aly said. "I remember now. I always thought it looked like a snow cone."

The elevator came to a stop. "Welcome to the O Deck," Malika told them. "You are now five hundred and twenty feet above Seattle."

They stepped out onto the open-air deck. Tourists stood by the guardrails, gazing out at the view. Some had binoculars; others looked through telescopes located on the deck.

It was early summer, but the morning air was chilly. Aly tightly wrapped the denim jacket she was wearing around her, and AJ zipped up her hoodie.

They followed Malika to the rail. The tall buildings and skyscrapers of downtown Seattle sprawled out below them, shadowed by Mount Rainier in the distance. Fluffy white clouds filled the lower sky, but they could still make out the snowy mountaintop.

"This is the south view from the tower," Malika explained. "From here you can see most of Seattle's business district, including the city's famous monorail."

They followed Malika around the circular deck. The view to the west showed more sparkling blue water, and the tall Olympic Mountains. To the north, ships sailed across the calm waters of the bay.

The east view was another sprawl of buildings, houses, and busy streets.

"I'm not sure, but I think I can see our old neighborhood from here," Carrie said. "Girls, I've got to take your picture!"

Aly and AJ posed in front of the rail, smiling for the camera. Carrie snapped the picture. When their mom put down the camera, the girls could see that her blue eyes were misty.

"To think, you were practically babies when we lived here," she said. "And now, you're all grown up, touring around the country!"

Jim cast a nervous glance at his watch. "Speaking of the tour, I've got a meeting with the management at KeyArena about your show," he said.

"And I've got a conference call soon," Carrie said. "I'm afraid we can't stay much longer."

"What's on our schedule?" AJ asked.

Jim flipped open his BlackBerry and skimmed through it. "You guys are free today."

"Then why don't we catch up to you later?" Aly asked. "I'd like to see more of Seattle while we're here."

"Sounds like a plan to me," Jim replied.

"Just don't tire yourselves out," Carrie warned. "You've got a busy week ahead of you."

"We'll be fine, Mom," AJ promised.

They all thanked Malika and headed back to the bottom of the Space Needle. Aly and AJ waved good-bye to Jim and their mom. Then they hailed a cab.

"Where to?" the cab driver asked.

"Is there a coffee shop nearby?" Aly asked.

The cab driver grinned. "You do know you're in Seattle, don't you?"

The cab driver let them out on a street in Capitol Hill, a Seattle neighborhood known for its coffee shops. They walked into the first shop they found, a cozy place with dark wooden chairs and tables and abstract art pieces on the walls.

They settled in at a table with their orders—a caramel latte for Aly and a mocha swirl for AJ. The warm aroma of the coffee started to wake them up even before they took their first sip.

"It's nice having Mom on tour with us," Aly said. "I think I'd miss her if she stayed at home."

"Me too," AJ agreed. "I just wish she wasn't so worried about us all the time."

"I think that's what moms are supposed to do, right?" Aly said.

Just then, AJ's cell phone rang. She took it from her bag and answered it. "Oh, hi, Lily," she said. She listened, nodding. "Okay. Well, thanks for checking."

"Was that about Claire's notebook?" Aly asked.

"They looked all over the theater, but they couldn't find it," AJ said. "That's too bad. This is starting to look more and more like a mystery."

"Maybe Claire left it at home," Aly said.

"Let's hope so," AJ replied. "But I've been thinking. Remember how angry that girl Heather was? What if she stole Claire's notebook because she was angry about losing?"

"That makes sense," Aly said. "People do strange things when they're upset."

Aly reached into her leather bag and took out her sketchbook. "Claire said it was purple, right? With a butterfly on it?" She began to make a sketch.

"Good idea," AJ said. "If this is another mystery, I'd better start taking notes."

She took her own notebook out of her bag, and Austin's blue flyer drifted out.

"What's that?" Aly asked.

"Austin gave it to me," AJ answered. "There's a big poetry slam tonight. Austin is going to perform. He said a lot of the contestants will be performing, too. He asked us to come."

Aly raised an eyebrow. "Both of us, or just you?"

"Both of us," AJ shot back. "Anyway, it might be interesting. We can get a better idea of what the contestants are like."

"And maybe ask around about Claire and her notebook," Aly said. "I think we should go. It'll be fun."

AJ picked up the flyer. "It doesn't start until ten o'clock tonight."

Aly grinned. "I guess we'll both need another latte, then."

CHAPTER FIVE:
A SURPRISING SECRET

"Wow, this place is packed!" Aly exclaimed.

The girls were standing outside of a small, brick-faced storefront. The black and red sign over the door read HOWL. Through the glass window they could see a small crowd of people gathered around a square stage.

"Might as well go in," AJ said. She glanced at her reflection in the mirror. She had paired a cream-colored tank top with her favorite pale-pink peasant skirt. Next to her, Aly wore a white blouse with skinny jeans.

The air-conditioning was pumping inside, but with so many people the club couldn't get truly cool. The dim lights helped, though. The brightest light in the place shone over the stage.

A boy with spiked green hair stepped in front of the microphone.

"Next up tonight, it's Heather Harris!"

The girls looked at each other. Could it be the same Heather who had been so angry with them yesterday?

It was. She had spiked up her brown hair with gel, so that it stuck out in all directions. She wore ripped jeans and a T-shirt with paint splattered on it.

"Whoa," Aly whispered.

"Austin did say that a lot of the contestants participated in the local poetry scene," AJ said. "But I guess I wasn't expecting to hear Heather."

"This poem is called 'Rage,'" Heather began. She took a dramatic, deep breath.

"You say I'm a loser?

What do you know?

You're lost.

Lost because you don't know something good when you see it."

Aly grabbed AJ's arm. "Something tells me we're better off if she doesn't see us," she whispered.

They made their way through the crowd, and discovered to their relief that the club was an L-shaped building. They turned a corner and found a room with a little more open space. People were sitting on big cushions on the floor, quietly chatting.

Aly sank down on a big orange cushion. "I can't believe it. Heather is so mad at us she wrote a poem about it!"

"I know," AJ said. "Rainbow told me she was dramatic. I guess she was right."

"Hey, you're not trying to hide from me, are you?"

The sisters looked up to see Austin standing over them. He pointed to a cushion between them. "May I?"

"Of course," AJ said. "We're not hiding from you. We were just a little, uh, surprised to see Heather here."

"I guess I should have warned you," Austin said. "The poetry scene here is pretty tight—and it can get pretty competitive, too. Everyone's really polite when a poet is onstage. But you should see what happens backstage. I stay out of it. I just do it because I love it."

"But you entered the songwriting contest," AJ pointed out.

"Well, yeah, but that's a great opportunity," Austin said. "And I'm not just talking about the scholarship. I just had to meet you guys."

"I'm curious," AJ said, changing the subject.

"Are all of the contestants part of the poetry scene?"

"Not all of us, but a few of us are," Austin replied. "Claire's here somewhere. She's really good. And Josh will be performing tonight. He's . . ."

"Standing right behind you," Aly said quickly, before Austin could say anything bad. "Hi, Josh!"

Josh gave them a nervous smile. He was wearing leather pants and a vintage rock T-shirt.

"I didn't know you two were going to be here," he said.

"Austin told us about it," AJ said. "Are you performing tonight?"

"I was going to," he said. "But now I'm not so sure. It makes me nervous having the judges here."

"We're not judging tonight, just having fun," AJ said. "Just pretend we're not here."

They heard the sound of applause from the next room. Heather's poem was done. Then the emcee announced Claire's name over the mic.

Austin held out his hand to AJ.

"Come on, you've got to see this," he said.

Claire stood in front of the microphone. Her long hair was unbraided, and hung in front of her face. She wore a gray T-shirt and a pair of khaki pants.

"This poem is called 'Lost,'" she said.

"Lost.

Every thought.

Every hope.

Every dream.

Lost.

Stolen.

My heart fills with despair . . ."

AJ noticed that Claire never even made eye contact with the audience as she read her poem. But they seemed captivated by her words. The club was absolutely quiet, except for the sound of Claire's voice.

When she was done, the silence was replaced with applause.

"Let me guess," Aly said to AJ. "That poem was about losing her notebook."

Claire quickly left the stage and went back to her lonely corner of the club. Aly and AJ followed her there.

"Claire, that was great," AJ said. "Really moving."

"Thanks," Claire said gloomily. "But it's probably the last poem I'll ever write. I looked at home for my notebook, and it's not anywhere. I have to sing two new songs for the contest tomorrow, and they're lost. Lost forever."

"Maybe you can try to remember them," Aly suggested.

Claire shook her head. "I tried. But my mind is empty. Whenever I try to think of them, nothing comes up."

"Then try again," AJ said gently. "Claire, you're a great songwriter. Aly and I would be really sad if you didn't show up tomorrow.

Just believe in yourself, and you'll remember."

This seemed to calm Claire down. "You really think I'm a great songwriter?" she asked.

The sisters nodded. "Definitely," Aly said. "You just need more confidence in yourself."

The club quieted down once more, and Austin took the stage. His smile seemed to light up the dark club.

"I wrote this poem for someone I just met," he said, looking in AJ's direction. AJ felt her cheeks flush.

"Oh, this is going to be good," Aly whispered.

Austin cleared his throat and began.

"She plays her guitar.

Blond hair streaming like rays of sunlight.

Each note fills my heart . . ."

Aly giggled. "Boy, he's laying it on thick, AJ."

Thankfully, the poem was short. Austin took a bow and jumped off the stage.

Then AJ felt a tap on her shoulder. She turned around to see Heather standing there.

"I need to talk to you two," she said.

AJ looked at Aly. Her sister shrugged. "We might as well clear this up."

They followed Heather to the back of the club.

"You guys think Austin is pretty great, right?" she asked.

"Listen, Heather, all of the contestants are talented . . ." AJ began.

"That's not what I mean," Heather snapped. "I'm just saying, you'd better be careful who you let win this competition, that's all."

"Heather, what are you talking about?" Aly asked.

"I heard about Claire's notebook," Heather said. "She's been talking about it all night. That's when I realized. I know who did it."

Heather's green eyes gleamed with anticipation.

"Did you see something?" AJ asked.

"I saw somebody open up Claire's guitar case and pick up the notebook," she said. She paused dramatically. "It was Austin!"

Contestant #6
Austin age: 17

CHAPTER SIX:
SLEUTHING IN SEATTLE

"Austin?" Aly asked, shocked. She looked at her sister. AJ's jaw had dropped.

"But he seems so sure of himself." AJ shook her head in disbelief. "Why would he have to stoop to something like that?"

Heather smirked. "Maybe you two aren't such great judges of character, either." Then she turned and stalked out.

Aly grabbed AJ's arm and pulled her close.

"Can we even believe what she's got to say?" Aly asked. "She is totally ticked off about being booted from the competition."

"It doesn't seem to fit with Austin's personality, but let's face it, we really don't know him that well," AJ answered. "The only thing we can do is ask him."

Aly agreed. The sisters walked back toward the front of the club. They didn't need to look far for Austin. He was waiting for them.

"There you are!" he said. "I was wondering where you were. Let's sit over here. We can have some privacy." He gestured toward three cushions in a dark corner. They all sat down.

"Did you like my poem?" Austin asked, smiling at AJ.

"It was very nice, but . . ." AJ faltered.

Aly jumped in. "But we need to ask you something. Did you take Claire's notebook?" she asked bluntly.

Austin looked surprised. The flirty smile he was aiming at AJ left his face. He shifted on the couch and looked down at the floor. "No, I didn't. Why would you think that?"

Aly and AJ exchanged glances. Something was up.

"Heather told us she saw you looking in the notebook," AJ said.

Austin snorted. He seemed to get some of his confidence back. "Heather? And you believe her? You saw how she flipped out after you read the results. She's just jealous and trying to make trouble," he said. Then he glanced up at the stage. "Hey, look," he pointed. "It's Josh."

Josh stood on stage. His eyes were closed and his head was down. The lights sparkled on his blond hair.

"To be me, you have to see me," Josh began. He continued to speak, putting a lot of feeling into his words. But once again, the girls thought it was kind of corny.

Austin looked at them and rolled his eyes. "That Josh. I wish he could get it together. Some nights, his poetry is really great. But when it's not good, it's really bad," he said.

"He does have real potential," AJ replied. "Especially writing melodies."

Aly let out a big yawn. "I think we'd better call it a night," she said. "It's been a long day and I'm beat." She and AJ got up.

"Good night," Austin said, standing up. AJ braced herself for some flirty remark, but he left quickly.

"I don't know who to believe, but something makes me think that Austin isn't being truthful with us," Aly said.

Now it was AJ's turn to yawn. "I agree. But right now the only thing I can think of is getting to bed!"

"Yummy!" Aly drooled. On a plate in front of her was a Belgian waffle loaded with strawberries and fresh whipped cream.

"To the max," AJ agreed. Her plate was piled high with eggs, fresh fruit, and pancakes.

They were eating breakfast at the hotel's restaurant. It was buffet-style and the serving tables were loaded with delicious treats. Aly put a forkful of waffle, strawberries, and cream into her mouth. She closed her eyes. "Mmmmmmmmm," she said. "Delicious."

"This is awesome, too," AJ said as she dug into her omelet.

"Wasn't Austin acting weird last night?" Aly asked after she swallowed her last mouthful.

AJ nodded. "I don't think he was telling the truth."

"Even if he is a horrible flirt, he seems like a nice guy," Aly said. "It makes me sad to think he'd do something like that."

"I know what you mean," AJ said. "But it was weird the way he got all flustered, and then tried to change the subject by talking about Josh. And he practically ran out when we were leaving!"

"But he said he didn't take Claire's notebook," Aly stated. "And we don't have any proof that he did, except that Heather said she saw him looking in it."

AJ sighed and put down her fork. "I wish there was a way we could prove for sure whether he did or didn't take it."

"I bet we can figure something out. We've already solved two mysteries," Aly said. "We helped Gigi find out who stole all those guitars in New York. And we figured who was sabotaging Sandra Peng's fashions in Miami."

"Yeah, we're the next Sherlock Holmes," AJ giggled.

Aly laughed. "We just need the magnifying glass—and a fingerprinting kit."

AJ stopped laughing. "Hey—a fingerprinting kit! That's not a bad idea. Remember the one we had when we were kids?"

Aly's eyes lit up. "That's right. And it really worked!" She paused. "Wait a minute. Are we seriously thinking about using a fingerprinting kit? That's a little . . . extreme, don't you think?"

"Hey, we keep getting into these detective situations, so we might as well get some detective equipment, right?" AJ reasoned. "Anyway, I think fingerprints are the best way to find out what happened to Claire's notebook. We can pick up a kit at a toy store. It's worth a try." She pulled her notebook out of her bag and opened it up.

"We'll need to check Claire's guitar case for fingerprints," AJ said as she wrote. "Then we'll have to rule out any prints on the case that are Claire's. If there are any strange prints, we can check them against Austin's."

"Sounds great," Aly said. "But how do we get Austin's fingerprints?"

"Hmmmm." AJ tapped her pen against her cheek. "I've got it! We've got an appearance this afternoon at that rock and roll museum, the Experience Music Project. All of the songwriting contestants will be there. We'll get his prints then!"

"I know Austin is crazy about you, but I don't think he'll let you take his fingerprints, especially if he is guilty," Aly responded.

"They'll be serving refreshments," AJ said. "I'm sure Austin will have something to drink. We can take the empty cup or can and get the prints from that. Maybe Jim can help us."

Aly shook her head. "It sounds crazy, but it just might work!"

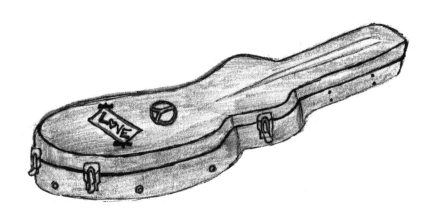

CHAPTER SEVEN:
A STRANGE PRINT

"Aly! AJ! What are you doing here?" Claire
asked as she opened the door to her apartment.

Aly and AJ had looked up Claire's address on
her contest entry form. Claire lived in the trendy
Belltown neighborhood, a mix of cool shops and
restaurants, newer condos and apartment buildings,
and older architecture. Her home was an old, red,
brick-faced building on a tree-lined street.

Aly and AJ both grinned a little sheepishly at

Claire. What had seemed like a great idea back at the hotel now seemed a little silly. They had stopped by a toy store and bought a fingerprinting kit. AJ clutched the bag in her hand.

Aly spoke first. "We feel really bad about your notebook. We want to help you find it."

"We thought if we could fingerprint your guitar case, we could find out if anyone else had touched it," AJ added. "I know it sounds silly . . ."

Claire's eyes grew wide. "That is so nice of you," she said softly. "I can't believe you guys are going to so much trouble to help me."

Claire's gratitude made the girls feel good about their decision. "We're happy to help," Aly said. "Can we see your guitar case, please?"

Claire led them to her bedroom, a small room on the second floor. The first thing Aly and AJ noticed about the room was that the walls were painted with deep purple paint. One whole wall was filled with bookshelves. Books spilled out onto the floor, but that was the only mess in sight. Claire's guitar case was propped up on the wall.

AJ set the guitar case on the floor, then sat down cross-legged in front of it.

"We'll concentrate on the handle and the lock, since that's what somebody would have touched to open it," she said. "Aly, give me the fingerprint powder, please."

"Wow, AJ," Aly said. "You sound so professional. Like you could be on one of those crime shows."

She handed AJ the fingerprint powder and brush. AJ dipped the brush in the powder, then brushed it on the shiny silver lock of the guitar case. She leaned down to get a closer look.

"Wow, it works!" she said. "There are a lot of prints here. A couple of clear ones, too."

"Try the handle now," Aly suggested.

AJ brushed the powder on the plastic handle, and more prints appeared.

"Great," AJ said. "Now we need to capture them."

The fingerprint kit came with a special sticky kind of paper. AJ put a piece of paper over one of the prints. The powder stuck to it, leaving a perfect impression.

"Cool," Aly said. "Let me try."

Soon they had a row of saved fingerprints.

"They all look the same," Claire remarked.

"Yes, but no two people's fingerprints are alike," AJ said. She took a magnifying glass from the kit and held it up to one of the prints. "There are ways to tell fingerprints apart from the patterns they make. Some have loops, or arches, or circles, called whorls."

She looked up at Claire. "We need to get a print from you to compare to the ones we just took."

Aly helped Claire roll her index finger on the inkpad that came with the kit. Then she pressed it onto a blank white card.

Claire began to giggle. "If anyone would have told me a week ago that I would be fingerprinted by Aly and AJ, I would have said they were crazy!"

AJ looked at the print under a magnifying glass. Then she looked at one of the fingerprints she'd found on the case.

"This is pretty tricky," she admitted. "You have to look really hard to see the details in a fingerprint. But Claire's print kind of stands out, because it's mostly arches. The line goes from one side of her finger to the other, see?"

Claire and Aly leaned in. Aly nodded. "You're right. It looks like a lot of the prints we took."

"Right," AJ said. "But then look at this one."

She pointed to another print she had taken from the case. The print had a big circle in the middle.

"Claire doesn't have any whorls," AJ said. "At least, not on her index finger. Let's check the others."

They checked the rest of Claire's fingers. None of her prints had whorls.

"So this print has to belong to someone else," AJ said. "Claire, has anyone else handled your guitar case?"

Claire shook her head. "No. I don't let anyone touch it, not even my mom. I'm real protective of my guitar."

Aly and AJ understood. Their guitars were very special to them, too. They had even named them—Artemis and Jonah.

"So the print must belong to the person who opened the case and stole the notebook!" Aly exclaimed.

"It looks that way," AJ said. "Now we just have to find out if Heather was telling the truth."

"I can't wait to see the Experience Music Project," Jim said. He was driving Aly, AJ, and Carrie. "I heard it is amazing."

"It is something to see," Carrie said. "The

Seattle Center Monorail runs right through it."

Aly and AJ had gone back to the hotel after their adventure at Claire's. They were going to be performing that afternoon, so they had to make sure they looked good. A bright lime-green halter top peeked out of the top and bottom of Aly's scoop-necked quarter-sleeve black T-shirt. She paired it with dark blue denim boot-cut jeans and a pair of black boots. Aly wore a deep purple v-neck top with ripped lace along the edges of the neckline. She wore a pair of vintage-looking jeans with black knee-high boots.

"It doesn't sound like any museum I've been to before," Aly said.

"It's very different, but neat. There are a lot of interactive exhibits. And you'll both love looking at all the rock and roll artifacts. I think you're going to go nuts over the Guitar Gallery. They've got Gibsons, Fenders, Les Pauls—even guitars from the 1700s," Carrie told them.

Jim parked the car and they all got out to walk. They were met with a strange sight. The museum building looked like it was made up of three parts. The center structure was a tall, shiny building that shimmered a coppery-pink in the sunlight. The two parts on either side looked like they had been built of giant sheets of metal that had curved like ocean waves. The girls had never seen anything like it.

"They really go for the space-age look in Seattle," AJ joked.

Once inside, a museum staff member gave them a quick tour of the Guitar Gallery before the reception began. They oohed and aahed over the guitars.

"I could spend hours here," Aly said.

"Me too. But we've got to make some musical history of our own," AJ replied.

The reception for the songwriting contestants was held in the Sky Church, an amazing room with soaring cathedral ceilings. It had a state-of-the-art sound system and a huge indoor video screen.

"I thought this was supposed to be low-key," AJ said nervously to Carrie.

"Yeah, I thought we were going to do an acoustic set," Aly said.

"Don't worry, you are," Carrie replied. "Don't let the environment psych you out. You'll do great."

They went onstage and checked out the microphones and tuned up their guitars. Soon the guests began streaming in. Amber was the first to arrive, decked out in black lipstick and a long black dress. A man and a woman were with her; Aly and AJ guessed they must be her parents. Her dad wore a colorful Hawaiian shirt, and her mom was dressed in pink from head to toe.

Aly looked at AJ and giggled. "I guess Amber is the rebel of the family," she whispered.

The room quickly filled up with a small crowd of contestants, their parents, and some members of the local press. All of the contestants had been invited, not just the finalists, but they were relieved to see that Heather wasn't there. They did see Bree and Henry; it looked like the two finalists had come together. They were deep in conversation in a corner.

Jim tapped Aly on the shoulder.

"Let's get this party started," he said.

The girls nodded and stepped up to the mics.

"Hey, everybody," Aly said. "I'm Aly."

"And I'm AJ," her sister joined in. "We just want to thank everyone who entered the songwriting contest. There's so much talent here in Seattle!"

The crowd responded with applause and a high-pitched whistle—from Austin, of course.

"All right, time to have some fun," Aly said.

The girls played a short acoustic set of some of their most popular songs, including "Potential Breakup Song" and "Like Whoa." The acoustics in the room were great, and the girls' voices came through pure and clean.

A local television news crew was there and filmed the performance. Afterward, Aly and AJ answered questions for the reporter about the contest and their upcoming concert in Seattle.

Finally they were finished and able to mix and mingle with the crowd. AJ pulled Aly aside.

"We've got to get Jim to help us," she said. "We'll distract Austin. Then Jim can grab his glass while he's not looking."

"Good idea," Aly said.

"Did somebody call my name?" Jim appeared behind them, smiling.

"You heard right," AJ said. "We need your help." She quickly explained their plan.

Jim raised an eyebrow. "You want me to steal his cup?"

"Not steal, exactly. You're collecting evidence," AJ said. "There's a plastic bag in my guitar case. Just place the cup in the bag, and we're good."

"While you're at it, you might as well get

cups from the other contestants, too," Aly said.

"Good idea," AJ said. "That print might not belong to Austin. That would mean one of the other contestants is guilty. Good thing I brought extra bags."

Jim shook his head. "Nowhere in my job description did it say I would have to do something like this." He laughed. "But I like the idea of playing detective. I think I can be really sneaky, too."

They moved into the crowd, searching out the contestants. The first they came across was Bree. Her curly dark hair framed her face. She looked casual, in a faded pair of jeans and a peasant blouse.

"You guys were great," Bree said. "You've got to give me some songwriting tips."

Bree was clutching a plastic cup. Luckily it was empty, giving Jim the perfect opportunity.

"Can I get you something to drink?" Jim asked politely.

"Thanks," Bree said. "That's very nice."

Jim took her old cup and went off to get her something new to drink. When no one was looking, he slipped the old cup into a bag. Then he wrote Bree's name on the bag.

Jim followed Aly and AJ as they spoke with each of the contestants. Henry put down his cup, so Jim was easily able to grab it up. He used the same trick on Josh and Rainbow that he did with Bree.

Then Aly and AJ approached Austin. He had a full cup of what looked like ginger ale that he hadn't taken a sip out of. He rested it on a nearby table.

"What are you doing tonight?" Austin asked AJ, his eyes sparkling.

"We're planning on staying in and relaxing," AJ said. "It's going to be a busy week."

"Are you sure you don't want me to show you the nightlife in Seattle?" Austin asked.

"Maybe another night," AJ said.

Then Austin turned and looked past AJ.

"Excuse me, what are you doing with my drink?" he asked. Jim had Austin's full cup in his hand and was walking away.

Aly and AJ looked at each other in a panic. Would Austin figure out what they were trying to do?

Austin's fingerprint

CHAPTER EIGHT:
A CHARMING LIAR?

Jim froze for a second. Then he snapped out of it. "Uh, there's a spider in it," he said quickly. "I, uh, saw it jump in."

"A jumping spider?" Austin asked, curious. "Let me see."

He stepped toward Jim, but Jim backed away. "It's really gross. I'll just get you a new ginger ale." Then he hurried off.

It was hard for Aly and AJ to keep from laughing.

"We'd better get going," AJ said. "Lots more people to see."

"Right," Aly said. "Later, Austin."

They found Jim in a private area behind the stage, bagging Austin's cup.

"A spider?" Aly asked, laughing.

Jim shrugged. "Hey, it worked, didn't it?" he said. "Maybe I'm not cut out for this detective thing after all."

"Don't worry," AJ said. "You did great. You got Austin, plus a few of the other contestants, right? We should be good."

"Right," Jim said. "I hope you two find what you're looking for."

"I think I am going to be seeing whorls and ridges in my sleep!" Aly complained.

The girls had gone back to the hotel after the reception. AJ had set up a mini-detective lab on the desk in the hotel room. She and Aly lifted prints from the five cups Jim had collected: Henry, Austin, Josh, Bree, and Rainbow. Then they started to compare them to the print from the guitar case. But it wasn't easy.

They checked Austin's prints first. His had a distinctive whorl in the center, just like the print on the case.

"That looks like a match," Aly said.

"I know," AJ agreed. "But we should check it against the others to make sure."

So at AJ's insistence, they compared all of the other prints to the print on the case. They saw lots of loops, whorls, and arches.

"I still think Austin's print looks the closest," Aly said.

AJ nodded in agreement. "Let's take another look."

They used the magnifying glass to examine Austin's print one more time.

"This definitely looks like a match," Aly said. "See that swirly thing under the whorl? And those arches on the right?"

"You're right," AJ said. "Nobody else comes close. I think we need to talk to Austin. It looks like Heather was telling the truth."

"I still don't think he'd do something like that," Aly said, frowning. "But you're right. We should find him. It's still early. Should we call him?"

"He'd probably think I was calling for a date," AJ said. "I'd feel bad getting his hopes up. Let's head down to Howl and see if he's there."

AJ's hunch was right. They found Austin standing outside the club, talking to Henry. Austin's eyes lit up when he saw them.

"Looking for me?" he asked, his voice full of hope.

"As a matter of fact, we are," Aly said.

Henry nodded. "I'll see you guys inside."

The tall boy went inside the club. Austin nodded after him.

"Lucky. He and Bree are going out. Love at first sight, he says." Austin looked at AJ. "I hear that happens sometimes."

AJ flushed a little. "Listen, Austin, I wish we were here for a different reason, but we need to talk to you about Claire's notebook."

Austin looked annoyed. "I already told you, I didn't take it."

"But we found something," Aly said. "Proof. Your fingerprint is on the handle of Claire's guitar case."

Austin looked shocked. "My fingerprint? But how . . ."

"Do you want to tell us what happened?" AJ asked.

Austin sighed. "You're not going to believe me," he said.

"Try us," Aly told him.

"I *did* open the guitar case," he said. "But I didn't steal Claire's notebook, I swear. I just . . . looked at it."

"Why would you do that?" AJ asked.

Austin ran a hand through his hair. "It was stupid, I know. It's just that Claire is my biggest competition in this thing. I mean, she's really good. I was just curious to see what she was planning. Then I felt weird about it, and I dropped the notebook. I left the guitar case open. Maybe somebody took the notebook then."

"But you could have told us this before," AJ said. "Why should we believe you now?"

Austin looked into AJ's eyes. "I don't expect you to. But it's the truth."

"It kind of makes sense," Aly offered. "If Austin left the case open, someone could have taken the notebook without leaving a fingerprint."

"I guess," AJ said, but she didn't sound convinced.

"Hey, do you guys want to go inside?" Austin asked. "We can have some coffee."

"No thanks," AJ said glumly. "We'd better go."

AJ walked down the street, followed by Aly.

"What's the matter?" Aly asked.

"I don't know what to believe," AJ said. "I thought the fingerprint would be solid proof. But now it seems like we just have more questions to answer."

Aly nodded. "Right. If Austin didn't do it, then who did?"

"That's what we need to find out," AJ said. "But I'm not sure how."

"We'll figure it out," Aly assured her. "We've got a pretty good track record so far."

AJ sighed. "I don't know. This might be our first unsolved mystery!"

CHAPTER NINE:
ROUND TWO

The next morning, Jim took Aly and AJ back to the theater. The second round of the competition was set to start. Each of the six finalists would perform one new song.

Aly and AJ went backstage to wish them luck. Bree was strumming her guitar. Henry was sitting on a stool next to her, staring at her, almost mesmerized.

Josh was studying his reflection in a mirror.

He looked handsome, as always. His blond hair was slicked back with gel, and he wore a leather jacket and jeans.

Austin was tuning his guitar in a corner. He gave Aly and AJ a nervous smile. Nearby, Claire was talking to Amber. She waved when she saw Aly and AJ.

"Hey, thanks for trying to help me," she said, when the sisters came over. "It meant a lot to me. I thought if you could go to all that trouble for me, I could at least try hard to recreate my songs. I worked all night last night. I think the song I'm going to do today is better than it was before."

"She's right. I heard it," Amber said. "She's going to be tough competition."

"We just wanted to wish everyone good luck," Aly said.

"I think things are going to start in a few minutes," AJ said. "Our manager, Jim, said there will be news crews covering this tonight. So do your best!"

The sisters headed back to their seats in the theater.

"That's amazing that Claire was able to recreate her song without her notebook," Aly said.

"I'm not surprised," AJ replied. "When I write a song, it stays with me, you know? I think Claire just needed to find some confidence in herself. I'm glad we could help. Although . . ."

"I know what you're thinking," Aly said. "Even though Claire has a song, her notebook is still missing. And one of the contestants had to have taken it."

"Right," AJ said, sighing. "I just won't feel right until this is all settled."

But there was no time to play detective; the competition was about to begin. A news reporter was waiting for Aly and AJ when they returned to their seats.

"So how will you judge the finalists today?" she asked them.

"We're looking for a well-rounded songwriter," AJ replied. "Someone with great lyrics but who can also create melodies and beats."

"And we're going to perform a song from the winner at our concert," Aly added. "So it has to be a song that speaks to us and who we are, too."

"It's going to be a tough choice," AJ said. "All of the contestants are great."

Jim walked up. "We'll have to wrap this up," he said. "The judging's about to start."

The reporter left just as Henry took the stage.

"I really liked the love song he sang last time," Aly whispered. AJ nodded.

Henry sang into the mic as taped music played in the background. It was another love song, and it sounded a lot like his first song.

"Hmmm," AJ said, writing in her notebook. "Not bad. But I wonder if Henry can do anything else?"

Austin took the stage next. He didn't look

nervous, like he had backstage. He had great positive energy, and he flirted with AJ once again as he sang. The song had a crisp rock beat and catchy lyrics about hanging out in the summertime.

"Austin's back to his old tricks," Aly teased when he left the stage.

"Maybe, but that song was hot," AJ said.

Bree came out, wearing a tank top, peasant skirt, and clutching her guitar. Her curly hair bounced wildly around her face as she played and sang.

"I'm taking my act on the road.

Don't know when I'll be home again . . ."

"Nice," AJ said.

Aly nodded. "Agreed. But not so original, maybe. It kind of sounded like a Rolling Stones song."

Then it was Claire's turn. She sang a song called "Crush," about a girl who had a crush on a boy in kindergarten, and then dates him in high school. She seemed more confident onstage, and her singing voice was louder this time.

"That's awesome!" Aly said when Claire was done.

"Way," AJ agreed. "I can so imagine us singing that."

While Claire's song was cheerful, Amber's was a lot darker. She got up close to the mic, her voice droning as she sang.

"Dark, dark, dark.

The lonely pits of my heart . . ."

"Cool," AJ remarked. "But could you imagine us singing that?"

"I honestly don't know," Aly answered. "I mean, we don't always sing happy songs."

"Yeah, but that was downright depressing," AJ pointed out.

Josh was the last finalist to perform. Like Henry, he sang to taped music in the background. He sang "Love Letter," a clever song about a boy who sends a love letter to the girl he secretly likes, but the wrong girl gets it, and they end up falling in love instead.

Aly and AJ were surprised.

"Wow, that was great!" Aly said.

"An awesome song," AJ agreed. "His lyrics have definitely improved."

It was time for Aly and AJ to narrow the six contestants down to three finalists. They looked at their notes.

"Claire is definitely in," Aly said.

"Right," AJ agreed. "And Henry is definitely out."

Aly nodded. "For sure. He needs to branch out a little more. What about Amber?"

"She's good, but I can't imagine singing one of her songs," AJ said. "So that leaves Bree, Austin, and Josh. We can only pick two of them."

Aly studied her notes. "I thought Austin and Josh were both great."

"Me too," AJ said. "But Austin . . ."

"There's no proof," Aly said. "And I *really* liked his song."

Aly sighed. "Okay. Are we on the same page?"

AJ nodded.

"Then let's call everyone out," Aly said.

The six contestants filed onto the stage. Aly and AJ stood up.

"This was a really tough decision," AJ said. "Even tougher than the last round. You're all great songwriters. But we're also trying to pick someone who can write a great song for us."

"So, our first finalist is Claire," Aly announced. "Great job."

Claire let out a happy squeal and hugged Amber.

"Our next finalist is Josh," AJ said. "Josh, you wowed us with your lyrics today."

Josh pumped his fist in the air.

"That leaves our third finalist," Aly said. She

saw that Henry and Bree were holding hands tightly. "Austin, we'll see you in the finals."

Austin let out a whoop and jumped in the air.

Henry and Bree hugged.

"You so deserve this," Amber told Claire. "I hope you win."

Aly and AJ watched them from their seats.

"No Heather-like outbursts this time," Aly said. "That's a relief."

"Maybe," AJ said. "But I won't be relieved until we solve this mystery."

Aly shook her head. "AJ, everything's working out fine. Maybe we should just let it go."

"We can't," AJ insisted. "The winner of this contest is going to get a great prize and lots of attention. I don't want to crown a thief by mistake!"

CHAPTER TEN:
LOST AND FOUND

Aly and AJ were beginning to get their stuff together to leave when Henry and Bree approached them.

"We just want to thank you for the opportunity," Henry said. "This was a great experience."

"It was so nice to meet you both," Bree said. "But before you go, I'd love to get some advice."

Aly and AJ chatted with them about writing songs and finding inspiration.

"I think it always helps to write about things you know about or have experienced," Aly told them. "People can always tell when a song comes from your heart."

Henry glanced at Bree. "I think I know what my next song will be about," he said, smiling shyly. Bree blushed.

They talked for a few minutes more, and then Henry and Bree left.

"They are so cute," AJ said to Aly as Henry and Bree walked away, holding hands. "It's nice that even though they didn't win the competition, they found each other."

Aly swung her purse over her shoulder. "You know, before we leave, I'd like to say good-bye to Amber, too."

"She might be backstage," AJ suggested. "Let's go."

They walked onto the stage and headed toward the backstage area. They could hear the contestants talking and AJ spotted a figure walking in the shadows, away from the stage door. The person had a sweatshirt on with the hood pulled up over his or her head.

"Hey," AJ murmured to Aly. "Who is that?"

"I don't know," Aly replied. She raised her voice. "Excuse me, can I help you?"

The person stopped and stepped out of the shadows. It was Heather!

"Oh, it's you two," she said.

"What are you doing here?" AJ asked.

Heather let out an exasperated sigh. "You know, we all had a life before Aly and AJ came to town. I know everyone here, remember? I came to see how they did in the competition."

Aly shook her head. "I didn't think you were tight with any of them," she said.

"We are a small community of poets and songwriters. I was curious to see who made it to the next round," Heather said. "And you know what?

89

I still think I'm better than all of them. You had the chance to sing one of my songs. Too bad you blew it. Later." She turned and stalked off the stage and toward the theater doors.

"Forget songwriting. She should really enter a Miss Congeniality contest," Aly said sarcastically. "I hope this is the last time we run into her!"

AJ looked thoughtful. "Did you believe that's why she was here? I think she might be trying to cause trouble."

"She definitely seems to have it in for this competition—and you and me!" Aly said.

Just then, a loud cry filled the air.

"What was that?" Aly asked. They pushed open the door and walked backstage.

Claire was standing over her open guitar case. In her hand was a purple notebook!

"My notebook!" she said. "Someone put it back in my guitar case!"

Aly and AJ hurried over.

"Are you sure it's yours?" AJ asked.

Claire opened the book and flipped through the pages. She looked up and smiled at the sisters.

"It is!" she said. "All the pages are here, too."

Austin patted Claire on the back. "I'm glad it turned up," he said.

Everyone began to talk as Amber and Josh came over to see what was going on.

"Maybe you just misplaced it," Josh suggested. "Like, it was stuck in the lining of your guitar case or something."

Claire shook her head no. "There are no holes in the lining and no room for something to get lost. Whatever the reason, I'm just glad it's back!"

"I'm so happy for you, Claire," Aly said.

"Even though I was able to remember my songs, I'm glad to have it back," Claire said. She smiled at Aly and AJ. "Thanks for all your help. Maybe whoever stole it got nervous when they

91

heard you guys were helping me look for it, so they returned it."

"I really think it just must have been stuck in your guitar case," Josh insisted. "I don't think any of us would have taken your notebook."

"We're just glad it's back," AJ said. "We've got to get going. We'll see you guys at the studio tonight, right?"

The finalists had been invited to watch the girls rehearse for their concert and share their songs with Aly and AJ's band.

"I'll be there," Austin said with a big smile. "I wouldn't miss it for anything in the world."

After saying their good-byes, Aly and AJ walked out of the theater and caught a cab.

"That's a relief," Aly said as she sank back into the seat.

"Even if Austin did take it, the notebook was returned, so there is really no crime, is there?" AJ asked hopefully.

"Or maybe that's what Heather was doing there sneaking around," Aly said. "Returning the notebook."

"Either way, the problem is solved," AJ said. "And we can concentrate on the contest—and our concert!"

After they relaxed for a little bit at the hotel, Jim dropped Aly and AJ off at a rehearsal studio for practice.

"Hey, guys!" Aly greeted the band as she walked into the room. "Did you miss us?"

"The bus was empty without you," the bassist, Malcolm, said. "But luckily we had Hello Kitty to keep us company."

Aly and AJ laughed. Their tour bus looked like a Hello Kitty factory had exploded inside. The cute cartoon kitten was on everything—pillows, blankets, dishes, even the shower curtain!

Jeffrey, who played keyboards and also served as the musical director for the tour, was tuning up along with Matt, the lead guitarist. Tommy, the drummer, sat at his drum kit, lightly tapping with his sticks.

Claire, Austin, and Josh walked into the room.

"I hope we're not late," Austin called. He gave that cute grin of his. "I wouldn't want to miss a second of this."

"It's like having a private Aly and AJ concert," Claire said. "I'm so excited."

Josh looked nervous. "I really want to hear some feedback about my songs."

"We'll get to that," AJ said. "But first, meet our band." She introduced the contestants to the band members.

Jeffrey stepped out from behind the keyboard. "First, we're going to run through our set for the concert," he explained to Austin, Josh, and Claire.

"So why don't you guys take a seat and get comfy. Afterward, we'd love to play some of your songs."

Jeffrey held up a large piece of poster board. It had song titles written on it in magic marker.

"I'm thinking the concerts in Miami and New York sounded great," he said. "Are there any changes you want to make to the set list?"

Aly and AJ looked at each other.

"I'm happy with it," AJ said.

"It works for me," Aly replied. "We'll just have to figure out when we should sing the winner's song."

They discussed it for a bit and then the girls strapped on their acoustic guitars and stepped in front of the microphones. Together with the band, they performed a quick sound check. Then they launched into the song they had been opening the tour with, "Potential Breakup Song."

"It took too long, it took too long, it took too long,
For you to call back,

And normally I would just forget that,

Except for the fact it was my birthday,

My stupid birthday."

After the stress of judging the contest and fingerprinting guitar cases, it felt relaxing to play and sing, backed by their band. They finished the song and went through the set list from beginning to end.

After the last song was played, Austin got to his feet and cheered and clapped. Josh clapped, too. Claire stood up, smiling from ear to ear.

"That was amazing!" she gushed.

"Wow! Thanks, guys," Aly said.

AJ smiled as she took off her guitar. "Thanks. But we're not done yet. Let's hear what you guys have got."

The band played a couple of songs from each contestant. Aly and AJ also had a chance to sing the songs, so they could get a feel for which one fit them the best. The guys from the band were really helpful, giving Josh, Claire, and Austin tips and advice.

"Thanks a lot," Austin said. He smiled at AJ. "It was really great to see you perform tonight. One day maybe you'll give me a private concert."

AJ giggled. "Maybe one day I will," she smiled.

Aly looked at her sister and raised an eyebrow. AJ blushed.

The contestants left, giving Aly and AJ a chance to talk about their songs with the band.

"I really like Claire's work," Tommy said. "Her lyrics were really insightful, plus she knows how to write great music, too."

"She is good," Jeffrey agreed. "But Austin's music has a certain something, like a catchy hook you just can't get out of your head."

"Yeah, I think Austin is my favorite," Malcolm said. "But Claire is talented, too."

Matt put his guitar on its stand. "I really dug Claire's work. She's a talented songwriter. Whether she wins this contest or not, she'll make a name for herself in the music industry."

AJ was scribbling in her notebook, trying to record the band's impressions of each contestant. She looked up.

"What about Josh?" she asked.

Jeffrey shrugged. "He's not bad, and he definitely has a flair for writing music. Except for that love letter song of his, his lyrics need work."

Matt nodded. "Josh isn't as well-rounded as the other two."

"So two votes for Claire, two for Austin, and none for Josh," Aly summed it up as AJ continued to write.

"Think of it this way," Malcolm said. "You can't go wrong with either Austin or Claire. Now you just have to pick one."

AJ looked up from her notebook. She looked at Aly.

"I don't think that's going to be easy!" she said.

CHAPTER ELEVEN:
BREAKING NEWS

"Ahhhhh," Aly said as she flopped on the couch in the hotel room. She had changed into her pajamas, an orange thermal top with a pair of pink pants that were dotted with images of cute bows and skulls. "I feel so comfy right now."

She had landed practically in her mother's lap. Carrie laughed and stroked her daughter's hair.

"You've had a long day," she said. "Just relax. Room service should be here soon."

Just then, there was a knock on the door.

"Perfect timing," Carrie said as she stood and walked to the door. A waiter in a fancy white and red uniform wheeled a cart into the room. Carrie directed him to the table in front of the couch and he began to place silver covered trays there. Carrie and Aly thanked him and he left.

AJ came out of the bedroom. Her hair was wet from the shower and she had on her pajamas, too, a black tee with a crazy squirrel face on it and a pair of orange pants dotted with peanuts.

"Mmmmm," she said as she inhaled. "Smells delicious. I'm starving!"

Carrie uncovered the trays for them. "Grilled chicken panini sandwiches," she said.

Aly and AJ pounced on the food. They sat back on the couch as they took big bites of their sandwiches.

"Hey," Aly said between bites of her food. "Let's turn on the news. The songwriting contest should be on. There were some reporters and a television crew there today."

Carrie grabbed the remote off the table and turned the TV on. After flipping through the channels, she found a local news station.

After talking about a robbery, a car accident, and the weather, the newscaster, a women with short brown hair, introduced the next segment.

"They were singing in Seattle today, as wannabe songwriters performed their songs for music sensations Aly and AJ. This sister act is judging the Seattle Young Songwriters Competition. The winner will have their song performed by Aly and AJ at KeyArena on Saturday night."

The camera had panned to images of Amber and Bree onstage performing, and to Aly and AJ sitting in the audience, watching. Then it cut away to a reporter standing backstage. She was interviewing the contestants before the competition had begun.

"Do you think you have a chance at winning?" she asked as she stuck the microphone in Claire's face.

"I feel like I already won," Claire said. She looked straight at the camera and spoke without blushing or stammering. "I was so shy when I began this process, but I'm a lot more confident now. It's all thanks to Aly and AJ. They've been just great to us!"

Carrie was beaming. "Girls, I'm so proud of you."

"Oh, Mom." Aly rolled her eyes.

The reporter interviewed Bree and Henry together. When Austin's face flashed on the scene, Aly shot a knowing smirk to her sister.

"Stop it!" AJ complained. But her cheeks got a little red.

Amber was interviewed, and finally, Josh. He was saying how he thought he had a chance at winning. AJ put down her sandwich and leaned closer to the television. She pointed at the screen.

"Look at Josh's pocket. What is that sticking out of it?"

Aly looked closely. Something was poking out of the inside pocket of Josh's leather jacket. And it was purple!

"It looks like the corner of a notebook—a purple notebook!" Aly said excitedly.

The scene changed. Now Aly and AJ were announcing the winners.

"The reporter interviewed Josh *before* the competition—before someone returned Claire's notebook," AJ said. "I'm starting to think that maybe that someone was Josh!"

"Why didn't we think of this before?" Aly asked. "I guess it makes sense. He had the same motive and opportunity as anybody else."

"Josh knows his lyrics need work. That's the feedback he keeps getting. He might have taken Claire's notebook to get some ideas, or even just to get rid of one of the strongest competitors," AJ suggested.

Aly nodded. "Claire was so shy in the beginning. Anybody might have thought that stealing her notebook would destroy her confidence and keep her from doing her best."

"If Josh knew his lyrics weren't good enough, sabotaging the competition might have seemed like a good idea," AJ said thoughtfully.

Aly looked right at AJ. "If Josh did it, then Austin was telling the truth."

"I'd feel a lot better about naming Austin the winner if he didn't steal Claire's notebook," AJ said, avoiding Aly's eyes. "We should try to find out if Josh really is responsible."

"If we get a chance, we should try and question him," Aly said. "If Austin is in the clear, not only can we name him the winner, but you can date him!"

"Aly!" AJ cried. She grabbed a pillow off the couch and threw it at her sister.

"Girls!" Carried interrupted. "You should get to bed. You've got another busy day tomorrow—starting with a photo shoot in the morning. Besides, I don't want you two to trash the hotel room!"

"Okay, Mom," Aly said. She put the pillow down. "AJ needs to get to sleep now—so she can dream about Austin." She turned and ran into the bedroom with AJ chasing after her, laughing.

Carrie chuckled and grabbed a pillow. "If I can't beat you, I may as well join you!"

CHAPTER TWELVE:
SOMETHING'S FISHY

"This place is huge!" Aly exclaimed. She looked around at the maze of buildings, streets, walkways, and alleyways that made up the Pike Place Market. It was early in the morning but the place was bustling with activity. Merchants were already open and selling fruits, vegetables, bread, flowers, and more to eager customers.

"Let's get our picture taken under the sign," AJ said as they stopped in front of the entrance to the farmers' market. The old-fashioned-looking sign next to the entrance had a big, round clock on it, and the words PUBLIC MARKET CENTER in big red letters.

Carrie laughed and pulled out her digital camera. "You're going to have your picture taken soon—at the photo shoot at Pike Place Fish Market."

"But that's for *Seattle Scene* magazine," Aly said. "This one is for our scrapbook."

The girls posed under the sign while Carrie snapped away.

"We need one of all three of us," AJ said.

A woman walked by carrying a bouquet of flowers.

"Excuse me, would you please take our picture?" AJ asked.

She smiled. "Sure," she said. "But you're going to have to show me how to work the camera. I can never figure them out."

"It's easy," AJ said as she showed her how to work it.

The woman stopped and gave a shriek. "Wait! You're Aly and AJ, aren't you? I can't believe it! I should have recognized you right away. My daughters have your pictures all over their room."

"That's us! And your name is?" Aly asked.

"Donna," she said. "Cassie and Leah are going to freak when I tell them about this. They both play guitar and want to perform together, just like you two."

Carrie asked, "Are they coming to the concert on Saturday?"

Donna shook her head. "It was sold out. We couldn't get tickets."

Aly and AJ smiled. They loved being able to surprise fans with tickets.

"We have some extra tickets, and we'd love for them to come," Aly said.

Carrie reached into her bag. "And I've got some right here with me," she said as she handed the tickets to Donna.

"Oh my gosh!" Donna exclaimed. "You all are so wonderful. Cassie and Leah are going to be so excited. Thank you so much! Now let me see if I can take your picture. I'm shaking so much it will probably come out all blurry!"

Donna snapped the photo and gave them all a big hug before leaving.

Carrie glanced at her watch. "We'd better hurry," she said.

They made their way through the market toward the main arcade, where Pike Place Fish Market was located. Aly and AJ had dressed to impress for the photo shoot, but were warned that there could be a "costume change" by the magazine's art director. AJ wore a fitted, white, off-the-shoulder top with a black vest over it, along with her favorite pair of jeans. Aly had chosen a baby doll tank that had a playful pattern in pink and black, with large straps and oversized, colorful buttons. Underneath it she wore a black three-quarter-length tee, paired with her favorite jeans.

They made their way through the market and stopped in front of Pike Place Fish Market. Huge whole fish were displayed on beds of ice. A glass counter held a colorful array of lobster tails, crab claws, scallops, fish fillets, shrimp, and more. A group of people from the magazine were waiting for them.

Carrie introduced Aly and AJ to Sasho, the art director; Monica, the photographer; and a young man named Tony who was there to do their hair and makeup.

A couple of chairs had been set up and Tony began to get them ready.

"You girls look fabulous!" Sasho said as Tony worked. The art director was stylishly dressed in black jeans and a vintage T-shirt. "I hope we'll be able to use your outfits for the shoot."

Aly and AJ exchanged glances. What exactly did Sasho mean by that?

The busy fish market was already starting to get

crowded with customers and workers. The workers wore large, orange, rubber overalls over their clothes and boots. Two of the guys began tossing a huge whole salmon back and forth, cracking jokes and putting on a show for the shoppers.

Sasho smiled at the girls. "I hope you guys like fish," he said. "Because I'd like to get a few shots of you doing the same thing."

"I like sushi," Aly replied. "But I'm not sure about that!"

"With our bare hands?" AJ asked apprehensively.

"Oh, you'll be suited up properly," Sasho said. "It's your choice."

Aly looked at AJ. "Why not?" she said. "It'll be fun!"

Tony put the finishing touches on their hair and makeup and the girls stood up. Sasho handed them each a pair of rubber overalls and a pair of big rubber gloves.

Aly giggled. "I guess we'll fit right in."

One of the workers approached them, smiling. He wore jeans and a flannel shirt under his overalls. A backward baseball cap topped his black hair, and his eyes were a clear shade of green.

"This is Shane," Sasho said. "He's going to show you how to throw fish."

"Follow me," Shane told Aly and AJ.

They walked to the front of the store. Shane grabbed one of the huge fish from the ice.

"It's not too hard," he said. "Why don't you try throwing it to me?" He handed the fish to Aly.

She wrinkled her nose. "I'll give it a try," she said as she hoisted the fish up. "Wow—it's heavy!" Aly tried to throw the fish but it slipped out of her hands, landing on the floor with a splat.

Shane picked up the fish and walked over to Aly. He placed the fish in her hands and stood behind her, guiding her arms with his. Aly couldn't help but notice how cute he was.

"So how long have you been a fish monger?" she asked.

"A couple of years now. I started in high school, and I'm going to college now. But I still work here part-time," he said. He released Aly's arms. "Now give it a toss. AJ, get ready to catch it."

Aly threw the fish to AJ, who was standing a few feet away. She caught it, staggering a little under the weight.

Shane looked at Aly and grinned. "You are the prettiest fish thrower we've ever had here."

"I bet you say that to all the girls," Aly laughed.

Monica, the photographer, had been setting up her camera while they practiced. Now she nodded to Sasho.

"Ready," she said.

"Great," Sasho replied. "Okay, girls. We want the shots to look really candid."

He directed the girls a little bit, telling them

where to stand and how to face the camera. When they were in place, he yelled, "Throw that fish!"

This time, AJ tossed the fish to Aly. It soared through the air, then landed with a thud in Aly's arms. She took a few steps backward, laughing.

"Perfect!" Monica said from behind the camera. "This is great stuff."

They played catch with the fish a few more times until Monica had enough shots to work with. Then they took off the big orange overalls and cleaned up. Sasho and Monica set up a few more shots, this time in front of a stall of fresh flowers.

"Those overalls were definitely a fashion no-no," Aly said after the shoot was over.

"I don't know; they looked really good on Shane," AJ teased as Shane approached them. AJ poked Aly in the side and made a little coughing sound. Aly ignored her.

"It was really nice meeting you," he said.

"Yeah, you too," Aly answered. "Thanks for the fish-throwing tips!"

"Anytime," Shane said. "I hope I get to see you again before you leave town."

"That would be great," Aly said.

"I've got to get back to work," he said. "Bye."

The girls said good-bye and Aly had to put up with some more teasing from AJ before Carrie appeared.

"Why don't you two grab some lunch?" she suggested. "I'm going to do some shopping. I haven't been here in ages!"

There were tons of places to choose from to eat. Aly and AJ walked around and finally decided on a little café that featured European sandwiches, soups, and salads. It was a beautiful, sunny day so the girls decided to eat on a bench outside. They split a roasted pepper and mozzarella sandwich on focaccia bread.

"Yummy," Aly said as she bit into the sandwich. "I think all that fish chucking made me hungry!"

They munched contentedly in the sun until AJ gave a little gasp.

"Look!" she said, pointing. "It's Josh."

It was Josh all right. His blond hair was a little messy-looking today. He had on a T-shirt and stood behind the counter of a take-out pizza restaurant. A young woman walked up to the counter. She had spiky brown hair and looked very familiar. When she turned slightly, Aly and AJ got a better look at her face. It was Heather!

They watched as Heather said something to Josh. He looked around before handing her a slice of pizza. Heather walked off with the pizza—without paying for it.

"What is that all about?" Aly asked AJ.

AJ frowned. "I didn't think Josh and Heather were such great friends that he'd risk losing his job just to give her free pizza," she said.

"We wanted to talk to him," Aly reminded her. "Here's our chance."

They finished the sandwich and walked up to the counter.

"Josh, hi," Aly said in a friendly way. "I didn't know you worked here."

Josh shrugged. "I don't like it too much, to tell you the truth. That's why I'm hoping to win the contest. It could start me on a new career and get me out of this place."

"Listen, Josh," AJ said. "We saw you being interviewed on the news last night. And we saw what looked like Claire's notebook in your jacket pocket."

"You must have seen my cell phone; it's blue," he said calmly. "Maybe it looked purple under the camera lights."

"So you didn't take her notebook?" Aly asked point-blank.

"No way," he said as he looked them right in the eye. "I keep telling everyone, she probably just misplaced it."

"We saw Heather over here, getting some pizza,"

AJ said. "And it looked like she didn't pay for it. I didn't know you two were such good friends."

A red blush began to creep up Josh's face. "Well, you know, ah, we've known each other a long time," he stammered. "Look, don't say anything about that, please. I could lose my job. Anyway, I've got to get back to work. I'll see you tonight at the competition."

He turned away from them and Aly and AJ walked away from the pizza stand.

"He seemed to be telling the truth about the notebook," Aly said. "But he got nervous when you asked about Heather. Could he have a crush on her?"

"On Heather? I don't think so. It didn't seem like that kind of nervous," AJ replied.

Aly sighed. "We need to go back to the hotel and get ready for the final round of judging. I hope we can get to the bottom of this before we pick a winner!"

CHAPTER THIRTEEN:
BACKSTAGE SABOTAGE

After a quick shower at the hotel to get rid of any lingering fish odors, Aly and AJ changed clothes and headed back to the theater. Their mom and Jim had come along to watch the final round of the songwriting competition.

Lily, the contest coordinator, led the girls, Carrie, and Jim to seats in the front row. Friends and family members of the contestants were also in attendance to see who would win. Aly and AJ spotted Henry and Bree sitting together, and Amber sitting a few rows behind them.

"I know you don't have an easy decision," Lily said. "But hopefully you'll be able to decide on a clear winner after this final round."

Aly and AJ wished it were that easy. Worrying about possibly giving the prize to a thief made everything so much harder.

Josh took the stage first. He must have changed and showered, too, because his hair was once again slicked back with gel. Instead of the T-shirt they had seen him in earlier, he was wearing a white button-up shirt tucked into a pair of pressed jeans. Over the shirt he wore a tuxedo-striped vest. As always, Josh looked very put together. But had he managed to get it together with his lyrics, too?

The music began to play. As always, Aly and AJ were impressed with the melody. Josh stepped up to the microphone, closed his eyes, and began to sing. He sang about feeling like he was on the outside of everything, always looking in.

"*Can you see me,*

Or do you look right through me?

Fading into the purple mist of morning."

The words were touching and surprisingly heartfelt. Aly and AJ exchanged surprised glances.

"Wow," Aly whispered. "I dig this song."

It was Claire's turn next. Instead of shuffling and staring at her feet, like she had in the first round, she walked with her head up and smiled shyly at the audience. Her red hair was loose, spilling in waves down her back. She wore a really cute plaid shift dress with a ruffled collar, black tights, and boots.

Amber let out a yell. "Go, Claire!" she screamed.

She stood in front of the microphone and swung her guitar strap over her shoulder.

"I'll be singing 'Prom Queen,'" Claire said. She began strumming her guitar and sang a song about a shy girl who nobody seemed to notice and who dreamed about becoming prom queen. Once again, Aly and AJ were impressed.

"I love it," AJ whispered to Aly.

Claire left the stage and the audience waited for the final contestant, Austin. A minute or so went by and still the stage was empty. Muffled shouting seemed to be coming from backstage. Lily quickly disappeared behind the curtains to see what was going on. Aly and AJ got up and followed her.

The sisters poked their heads backstage. Josh and Claire were standing next to Austin, who was fuming.

"What happened?" Lily asked him as Aly and AJ walked into the room.

"My guitar is totally out of tune!" Austin yelled. "I was getting ready to go onstage and luckily I strummed my guitar first. It sounded horrible so I went to tune it. But someone has loosened the screws on the back of the headstock." Austin flipped his guitar over to show them.

"Can't you just tune it now?" Lily asked.

Austin shook his head. Aly took the guitar from him and examined it. "You're right. The screws are loose. You need a screwdriver to fix it before you can retune it," she said.

"This was no accident." Austin was mad. "The only way for this to happen is if someone took a screwdriver and loosened the screws."

"He's right," AJ said. "Someone must have done this on purpose. He's lucky he found out before he went onstage."

Claire held her guitar out to Austin. "Use mine," she said. "I just finished playing it and I know it's in tune."

"Is everything okay?" Jim asked as he walked into the room.

"Not really," Aly said. They grabbed Jim by the arm and led him to a quiet corner, explaining what had happened.

"Can you look around and see if Heather is here anywhere?" Aly asked. "She's been seen sneaking around here before. She might have had something to do with Austin's guitar being sabotaged."

"I'm going to add super-spy to my resume when we're done in Seattle," Jim joked. "I'll take a look around."

Austin seemed to be calming down and was getting the feel of Claire's guitar, so Aly and AJ headed back to their seats. The audience had grown restless, and a lot of people were talking to one another, wondering what was going on.

"Is this proof that Austin is innocent?" Aly asked AJ as they walked.

AJ shrugged her shoulders. "This is the most confusing mystery yet. The notebook is stolen. Then someone puts it back. Heather is sneaking around and getting free pizza from Josh. Now someone has messed with Austin's guitar. I don't know what to think!"

"Maybe Austin is some kind of evil genius," Aly suggested. "He might have sabotaged his own guitar to make us think that he is innocent."

AJ sank into the red velvet theater seat and sighed. "I'm totally perplexed."

They filled Carrie in on what was happening backstage. She shook her head.

"That's a shame," she said. "These kids have real talent. They don't need to stoop to cheating."

The audience quieted down as Austin finally took the stage. Looking at him, no one would guess that he'd been so upset a few minutes ago. He looked cool, calm, and confident—not to mention handsome. His long brown bangs were styled to the side and he had on an olive ribbed sweater with a half-zipper at the collar. Underneath he wore a black T-shirt and a pair of really nice faded jeans.

He held Claire's guitar and began to play while he sang. Aly and AJ loved the cute song he had written, an upbeat number about him and his friends driving around town on a Saturday night. Once again, his showmanship was the best. He worked the stage and the crowd, getting loud applause from the audience when his number was over.

"This is not going to be easy," AJ said.

Aly nodded in agreement. "They were all fantastic tonight," she said.

"But one of them could be a cheater," AJ added.

Aly groaned. "What are we going to do?" she asked.

CHAPTER FOURTEEN:
THE FINAL CLUE

Lily took the stage.

"Aly and AJ have a big decision to make," she announced. "We're going to take a fifteen-minute intermission so they can choose a winner."

Then Lily led the sisters to a small office inside the theater. "I'll give you guys some privacy," she said, closing the door.

Aly shook her head. "I can't believe we have to pick just one winner!" she said. "This is going to be tough."

AJ opened up the folders Lily had given her and Aly at the start of the round. Each folder held a photo of the contestant, plus music and lyrics sheets for each song the contestants had performed. AJ spread out the folders for Josh, Austin, and Claire on a folding table in the office.

"All right," she began. "The band likes Austin and Claire the best. It's going to be tough to choose between the two of them."

"But Josh was really good tonight," Aly pointed out. "I dug that sound. What were those lyrics? The purple mist of morning?"

AJ found the lyrics sheet. "Here it is," she said. Aly picked it up and started singing the song.

"Can you see me,

Or do you look right through me?

Fading into the purple mist of morning."

Aly put down the lyrics sheet and frowned.

"What's wrong?" AJ asked. "That sounded nice."

"I know," her sister said. "But there's something . . . where's the sheet for Claire's prom song?"

Aly shuffled through the papers in Claire's folder until she found what she was looking for. She quickly scanned the words on the page.

"Here it is!" she cried finally. "Listen."

"I'm fading into the background.

Surrounded by my dreams.

Shadowed by the purple mist of morning."

AJ gasped. "Are you kidding? I didn't know those words were in Claire's lyrics, too," she said. She grabbed the sheet from Aly. "This is too much of a coincidence. How could Josh and Claire both have the same phrase in their songs? I mean, who thinks up a phrase like 'purple mist of morning'?"

"Someone who likes purple," Aly said. "Someone who is good with lyrics."

AJ nodded. "I think we've finally figured things out," she said. "Come on. I want to clear this up before we make our final decision."

The girls left the office and headed for the backstage area. They saw Jim walking down the hall, headed for them. Heather walked by his side.

"I found her hanging around the backstage door, just like you thought she might be," Jim said.

"So?" Heather protested. "Is there a law against that? I haven't done anything wrong here!"

"You might not have done anything wrong, Heather," AJ said, looking her directly in the eyes. "But I think you know who did!"

CHAPTER FIFTEEN:
CONFESSION

Heather looked down at her leather boots. "I don't know what you're talking about," she said.

"Yes, you do," AJ said. "You know that Josh stole Claire's notebook. You were hanging around backstage the day the notebook was returned, and you saw Josh do it. That's why he's giving you free pizza. It's his price for keeping you quiet."

"Listen, I—" Heather began. But then the angry look on her face faded. "I . . . I shouldn't have gotten messed up in all of this. I was upset. You'll have to talk to Josh."

"We will," Aly said. "And I think you'd better come with us."

Heather reluctantly followed them backstage. Claire looked up, her face pale and nervous, when she saw them.

"Are you going to tell us who won?" she asked.

"Not yet," AJ said. "We have something to straighten out first. One of you is going to be disqualified—for cheating."

Claire let out a gasp. Josh's face looked bright red. And Austin looked perplexed.

"What do you mean?" he asked. "Not the notebook again!"

"Yes," Aly said. "We know who took it. It was Josh!"

"I don't know what you're talking about," Josh said coolly.

AJ began to pace back and forth across the room. "You saw Claire's open guitar case the night of the first round," she said, ignoring his protest. "You knew Claire was a favorite to win the contest. So you stole the notebook. You thought you would shake her, maybe even make her quit."

"But you didn't," Aly jumped in. "Claire did even better in the second round. You knew we were looking for the notebook. So you returned it. And you decided to sabotage Austin next."

"You loosened the screws on Austin's guitar," AJ said.

Josh shook his head. "You guys have no proof," he said.

"But we do," Aly said. She held up the lyrics sheet for his song. "We knew it was you when we saw your lyric—'the purple mist of morning.'"

"Hey, that's *my* lyric," Claire said.

"Exactly," AJ said. "Josh must have seen the words in your notebook and used them himself."

Josh's face was starting to turn red again. "How do you know Claire didn't steal the lyric from me?"

"For a couple of reasons," AJ began. "Number one, Claire's favorite color is purple. Number two, that's a really cool lyric—something that Claire would write, not you. And—"

"Number three, we have a witness," Aly interrupted. "Heather saw you put the notebook back in Claire's case."

Heather looked down at her boots again.

Then Jim stepped between them. He held Josh's leather jacket in his hand. "And something tells me if someone were to check your pocket, they'd find a screwdriver there—a screwdriver that fits the screws of Austin's guitar."

"All right! All right!" Josh cried out. "Obviously I can't win here. I did it. I stole Claire's notebook. I messed up Austin's guitar."

Aly and AJ grinned at each other.

Josh ran a hand through his hair. "I didn't mean to," he said, sinking down into a chair. "I just wanted to win this so badly. I knew I didn't have as much of a chance as some of these other guys. And Claire's notebook was out in the open . . . I just grabbed it. I didn't even think. I thought maybe I could get some inspiration from it."

Aly frowned. "Like the 'purple mist of morning'?"

Josh shook his head. "Honestly, I didn't steal that on purpose. I must have read it and it got stuck in my head . . . I thought it was mine." He looked like he was going to cry. "I can't believe I blew my one chance."

Jim walked up to Josh and gently lifted him up. "Let's get out of here," he stated. "We don't have to mention anything about this until the contest is over."

The sisters nodded. A cheating scandal would ruin a happy moment for the other two finalists.

"So does that mean the contest is over?" Claire asked.

"Not yet," AJ said. "Aly and I have to pick a winner."

Aly looked at her watch. "We'd better do it quickly."

They ran back to the office.

"Hey, we were great back there," Aly said. "Laying out the mystery like that. I imagined I was a detective on a TV show. I liked how you were pacing back and forth. Nice touch."

"I thought so," AJ said. "But now that the mystery's solved, we've got to choose a winner. Is it Austin or Claire?"

"Austin's a better performer," Aly pointed out. "But this is a songwriting contest, not a performing contest."

"He's a good songwriter, too," AJ said. "But so is Claire."

"Let's look over their songs again," Aly suggested.

They quickly read the lyrics sheets. They looked up at the same time.

"I guess it's obvious," Aly said.

AJ nodded. "It is," she said. "But I think I have an idea that will make everyone happy."

Singing in Seattle

CHAPTER SIXTEEN:
SHOWTIME

"The KeyArena is proud to present Aly and AJ's special guest!" the announcer blared over the speaker. "Please welcome Austin!"

Thousands of Aly and AJ fans cheered as Austin took the stage. They had never seen him before, or even heard of him, but he was a cute teenage boy—and a friend of Aly and AJ's. That's all they needed to know.

"Hello, Seattle!" Austin called out. The crowd

cheered again. He grinned, then launched into his song.

The crowd loved it. Austin gave a great performance, dancing across the stage as he sang and played his guitar. When the song was over, he waved and ran off the stage.

Aly and AJ were waiting for him.

"Wow, what a rush!" he said, sweat pouring down his face. "I can't believe you guys get to do that all the time."

"It's a great feeling," AJ agreed.

Austin unstrapped his guitar. "I have to thank you guys again for letting me do this. It's completely awesome."

"We wish there could have been two winners for the contest," Aly said. "But we had to pick one. We liked Claire's songs a little better. But you're an awesome performer."

"We'll try to help you get a break whenever we can," AJ said.

Austin gazed out at the cheering crowd. "I think this is a pretty good start," he said. "It makes me feel a lot better about losing the contest."

He looked at AJ. "I'd feel even better if you'd go out with me after the show," he said.

AJ smiled. "Sure," she said as Aly raised an eyebrow. "Meet me at our dressing room later."

"Thanks," Austin said. His smile could have lit up the entire arena.

Next, some stagehands handed Aly and AJ their electric guitars. Jeffrey and the other bandmates appeared.

"Ready to rock?" Jeffrey asked.

"Let's do it," the girls replied.

They ran out onstage. The arena erupted in applause and screams. Aly and AJ took their places behind the two microphones at the front of the stage.

"It's great to be back in Seattle!" AJ yelled.

The crowd went wild.

"We're going to open the show with a special song," Aly told the fans. "It was written by the winner of the Seattle Young Songwriters Competition, Claire Hayden."

AJ strummed a chord on her guitar. Tommy started a slow beat on his drums. Then the girls launched into Claire's song, "Prom Queen."

The crowd loved the song. People were standing up and dancing, and by the second chorus, they were even singing along. Aly and AJ smiled at each other across the stage. They had picked the right song.

They played the song's final chord, and the audience clapped and cheered. Aly glimpsed Claire standing backstage. She had a look of stunned happiness on her face.

Aly walked to the side of the stage. "Seattle, meet your songwriter, Claire!"

Aly motioned for Claire to come onstage. She hesitated for a minute. The applause just got louder.

"Come on, Claire!" AJ called.

Claire took a deep breath and stepped out to face the crowd. She gave a shy wave, then hurried back to her hiding place.

The concert had gotten off to an amazing start, and the rest of the show went just as smoothly. The crowd's energy was strong and upbeat all night.

After the show, the girls gulped bottles of water in their dressing room. Then AJ started to fix her makeup in the mirror. There was a knock on the door.

"That must be Austin," she said. "Come in!"

Austin stepped inside. "Great show, guys," he said. "AJ, where would you like to go?"

"Anyplace but Howl," AJ said. "I think I've had enough drama for one week."

Austin laughed. AJ turned to Aly. "I feel bad leaving you here alone. Do you want to come with us?"

Aly smiled. "You don't have to worry about me." She looked past AJ, toward the dressing room door.

A boy with brown hair and green eyes stood there, holding a bouquet of daisies.

"Hi, Shane," Aly said.

Then AJ remembered—it was the cute guy from the fish market. "Hey, I almost didn't recognize you without your orange overalls," she joked.

Shane blushed. "My mom says I clean up pretty nice," he said.

"Would you guys mind waiting outside for just a minute?" Aly asked. "We both need to freshen up a little more."

"Sure," the boys answered at once. They left and closed the door.

AJ picked up a hairbrush. "This was a pretty crazy week. I'm relieved that everything turned out okay."

"Me too," Aly said. "Playing detective is fun.

But I'm glad the only mystery we're faced with now is whether we'll have a good time on our dates tonight."

AJ grinned. "That's one mystery I look forward to solving!"